The Tsar & the Amazing Cow

by J. Patrick Lewis ◆ *pictures by* Friso Henstra

Dial Books for Young Readers *New York*

Published by Dial Books for Young Readers
A Division of NAL Penguin Inc.
2 Park Avenue
New York, New York 10016

Published simultaneously in Canada by Fitzhenry & Whiteside Limited, Toronto
Text copyright © 1988 by J. Patrick Lewis
Pictures copyright © 1988 by Friso Henstra
All rights reserved
Design by Atha Tehon
Printed in Hong Kong by South China Printing Co.
First Edition
W
1 3 5 7 9 10 8 6 4 2

Library of Congress Cataloging in Publication Data
Lewis, J. Patrick. The tsar & the amazing cow.
Summary: A cow's magic milk restores youth to her owners
and brings back the happiness they had tragically lost.
[1. Folklore — Soviet Union.]
I. Henstra, Friso, ill. II. Title.
PZ8.1.L4444En 1988   398.2'45297358'0947   [E]   86-29255
ISBN 0-8037-0410-0
ISBN 0-8037-0411-9 (lib. bdg.)

To my mother and father J.P.L.

To my granddaughter, Tessa F.H.

In the heart of a faraway Russian village there lived an old peasant couple, Maria and Stefan. Long ago they had three daughters, who died in the green time of their lives. Elenichka drowned when she was ten. At twelve Mashenichka died of the plague. Baby Irinoushka once wandered too far from home. Day and night they searched the birch forest. She was never found.

The loss of their daughters leaned on Stefan and Maria like fallen trees. Still they made their way in the small world of the village. They owned a cow—Buryonka was her name—and they loved her like family. Though Madame Luck had always skipped too quickly past the old couple's door, it happened that this was Ivanov's Day, which marked midsummer. For Maria and Stefan and the cow it would begin a time like no other.

As the sun fell behind the fields Stefan left the cottage for his evening visit with Buryonka. There in the stall he milked her, and he talked to her cheerfully. And indeed it seemed as if the cow were actually listening, as she had listened to all the stories of all the evenings past. Her flanks shuddered; her tail whisked; her eyes blinked. Otherwise she was silent.

But Stefan's high spirits soon disappeared. Something had reminded him of Maria's grief for their lost daughters. It had been years since he had heard his wife's laughter. "Is there nothing I can do to ease her sorrow?" he said.

Suddenly the cow turned her head—and spoke.

"Drink the milk, Master. It is more than milk now. It is magic."

Stefan fell over backward off his stool. Trembling with excitement, he lay in the straw, dazed by the cow's words. But Buryonka said nothing more.

Finally he bid his cow good night and, carrying the pail of milk with great care, returned to the cottage.

When he explained to Maria what had happened, she said he must have stolen all the foolishness in the village and stuck it under his cap.

"Well, we will see soon enough!" Stefan replied.

The cottage was thick with the summer's heat and so, after drinking a glassful of the cow's milk, the couple went to bed.

When they awoke, everything had changed. For as night turned to day the old became the new. Maria's white hair had turned to silky black; her wrinkled skin was smooth. And she saw in Stefan not the bent back of a Russian peasant, gone creak in old age, but the strong and supple young man she knew long ago. They smiled the smiles of thirty-year-olds, which was exactly how young they had become.

"Buryonka. It's Buryonka!" shouted Stefan. He grabbed Maria by the hand and raced out to the stall, where his faithful cow was waiting.

Now the magic milk could not be kept a secret for long. Young Stefan told a neighbor, who told the village, and soon the cow's fame flew like a legend across the country until it reached St. Petersburg itself.

Two months later the young peasant couple sat at their kitchen table in despair. The wicked Tsar had heard of the miracle and had sent his men to bring the little family before him.

"What is to be done?" asked Maria mournfully.

Just then Buryonka nudged her head through the open window of the cottage. "Mistress, we *must* go to St. Petersburg," she said. "It's our only choice . . . and our only hope. When the Tsar's men come, take three scarves with you—a red, a green, and a yellow one. Stay close and listen to me."

"Why?" Maria asked the cow. "What can be gained?"

But Buryonka said nothing more.

Next morning twenty soldiers rode into the village. They led Buryonka into a huge cart pulled by three white horses. Maria and Stefan got in behind her and took their seats. Immediately the Tsar's Imperial Guard began the long journey back to St. Petersburg.

As they crossed the rickety bridge beyond the village Buryonka shouted,
"Mistress, the red scarf — throw it in the river!" Without anyone seeing her,
Maria dropped the scarf in the water below.

They passed through the old cemetery.

"The green scarf," boomed the cow. "Throw it on a grave!" No one noticed the green scarf that fluttered out of the cart.

A dark wood loomed ahead. Over the clatter of horses' hooves came the cow's cry. "There, among the birches, Mistress. Let the yellow scarf go!" And so Maria threw the yellow scarf.

Then Buryonka curled up in the straw and fell asleep.

Three days later they came to the Tsar's Grand Palace. The guards led the way into the Great Hall. How magnificent it was! Ladies in dazzling gowns and gentlemen in fine uniforms mingled before the throne. The food spread along the royal tables could have fed a village for a year.

"The records show," said the Tsar, "that you are both seventy years old, but any fool can see that you're not a day over thirty." He scowled fiercely.

"It is said that good fortune stands there beside you. For that cow I offer you ten head of cattle, a hundred hectares of the richest land in the Black Earth region, and a fine dacha to replace your hut."

Stefan and Maria trembled at the thought of a bargain that would take away their cow. They froze with fear.

"Bring the beast here," the Tsar thundered, "or I will have your heads!"

But already Buryonka was ambling fearlessly to the throne. She let the guards milk her, and the milk filled a huge vat.

The Tsar grabbed a bowl and dipped it in the vat. He finished one bowlful. His bald head grew thick with hair, and the whiskers darkened on his chin. He stopped to admire his thirty-year-old body.

"Aaaahhh!" he exclaimed. "All of Russia can rejoice that I am young again." Then he lifted the bowl once more.

But greed drove him to drink too much of the magic milk. He drank another bowlful. Then another. And another.

He grew younger—a Tsarevich—and smaller still—an infant Tsar—and POOF! He was gone.

Instantly the throne held another old man, the Tsar's father, as evil as his son. Time raced backward—faster, faster—as he too grew down to a boy, a baby, POOF!

Two, three, four generations swept away in a minute! When the Tsar's great-great-great-grandfather appeared, the ancient ruler looked around the court and shook his head.

"What in the world is a cow doing in my Palace? And this vat of milk? And you, peasants, how did *you* get here?" But the new old Tsar was in no mood to listen to anyone but himself. "Go back to your village the same way you came, and be quick!"

Just then Maria recalled the cow's mysterious words at the cottage window: "We *must* go to St. Petersburg . . . our only hope." What more could be hoped for than to escape the wicked Tsars? But there was no time for wondering. Maria hurried Buryonka into the cart and jumped in beside Stefan. And the gleaming white horses galloped homeward.

Three days had passed when Buryonka raised her head and bellowed, "Look sharp, Mistress, birch trees ahead!" Maria remembered the yellow scarf, but from that moment to this she could not imagine why she had thrown it to the wind. There in the dark glade danced a little girl in a yellow dress.

"Irinoushka! Can it be?" cried Maria. Indeed it was their baby daughter, lost in the woods so many years ago. When Stefan swept her up into the cart, she clapped her hands and sat straight up on Buryonka's back.

They came at length to the cemetery. On her own headstone sat the second daughter, Mashenichka, in a lovely green dress. Free from the plague that had taken her, she rushed to join the family, and the cart moved on.

"Bridge ahead!" announced Buryonka. "Look there, along the riverbank!" Barefoot Elenichka, the oldest daughter, who had drowned so long ago, was splashing in the shallow water. When she saw the huge cart, she gathered up her red dress and ran to meet it.

As the horses drove onward Maria clung to her found family and Stefan whispered a thank-you in Buryonka's ear.

Soon they came within sight of the cottage. And there they began the green time of their lives once more.